To my son Thomas, my nieces Naimi and Tainá
and to everyone who can still believe in dreams. s.m.

For my daughter Miriam: Shine Miriam, shine! g.f.

minedition

North American edition published 2014 by Michael Neugebauer Publishing Ltd. Hong Kong

Text copyright © 2011 by Sueli Menezes
Illustrations copyright © 2011 by Giuliano Ferri
Original title: Nino, das Glühwürmchen
Rights arranged with "minedition" Rights and Licensing AG, Zurich, Switzerland.
Michael Neugebauer Publishing Ltd., Unit 23, 7F, Kowloon Bay Industrial Centre,
15 Wang Hoi Road, Kowloon Bay, Hong Kong. e-mail: info@minedition.com
This book was printed in January 2014 at Beijing AF printing.
Opto-Mechatronics Industrial Park No.2, ZhengFu Road, Tong Zhou District, Beijing, China
Typesetting in Esprit
Color separation by HiFai, Hong Kong
Library of Congress Cataloging-in-Publication Data available upon request.

ISBN 978-988-8240-75-3

10 9 8 7 6 5 4 3 2 1
First impression

For more information please visit our website: www.minedition.com

Sueli Menezes

# Nino's
# Magical Night

with pictures by Giuliano Ferri

minedition

Nino, the little firefly, was exhausted.
He and his friends had been shining in the
forest all night long.

But he just couldn't sleep. He was thinking about something.

He asked his mother, "We all make such a beautiful light, don't we? But could we ever light up the night the way the moon does?"

Nino's mother thought for a minute and then said,
"That's a funny question, Nino!
What makes you ask that?"

"Well," replied Nino, "all the animals in the jungle think the moon is so wonderful for making the night so bright, but they never seem to notice us."

His mother smiled. "Nino, my dear, we have our own important job to do. The moon makes the night bright, but we fireflies make it beautiful – and magical – when we glow through the night."

But this wasn't good enough for Nino. "I bet we could do as good a job as the moon, couldn't we?" But his mother said it was time to sleep.

High above them, the moon had been listening. He could see that Nino was a determined little firefly, and he wanted to make him happy.
The moon had an idea.

The next night, the moon called to Nino, "Nino! I'm a bit tired. I need a rest. Just for one night, I'd love to sleep behind the mountains. Could you help me?"

Nino was so excited. This could be his big chance.
"I've always dreamed of us fireflies lighting up the night!"
Could they really do it? He thought and thought about it.

The following evening, Nino gathered all the fireflies together. "I have something important to tell you.
Our friend the moon is feeling tired and needs a rest. He's asked us if we could light up the darkness for one night."

The fireflies looked very worried. "How can we do that?" they asked. "We are so tiny!"

An old firefly, who had always dreamed of lighting up the night, suddenly called out, "Of course we can do it, if we all try!" Slowly, one by one, they agreed that they would try their best.

And so this is what happened. The very next night the moon went to take a rest. It became very dark with no moonlight, and the animals started to worry.

Very quietly, the fireflies gathered together in the center of the forest. Nino asked them to move close together and form a great ball of fireflies.

Then, just as the moon would do,
they rose slowly into the sky.

What a beautiful sight they became as they rose
higher and higher.

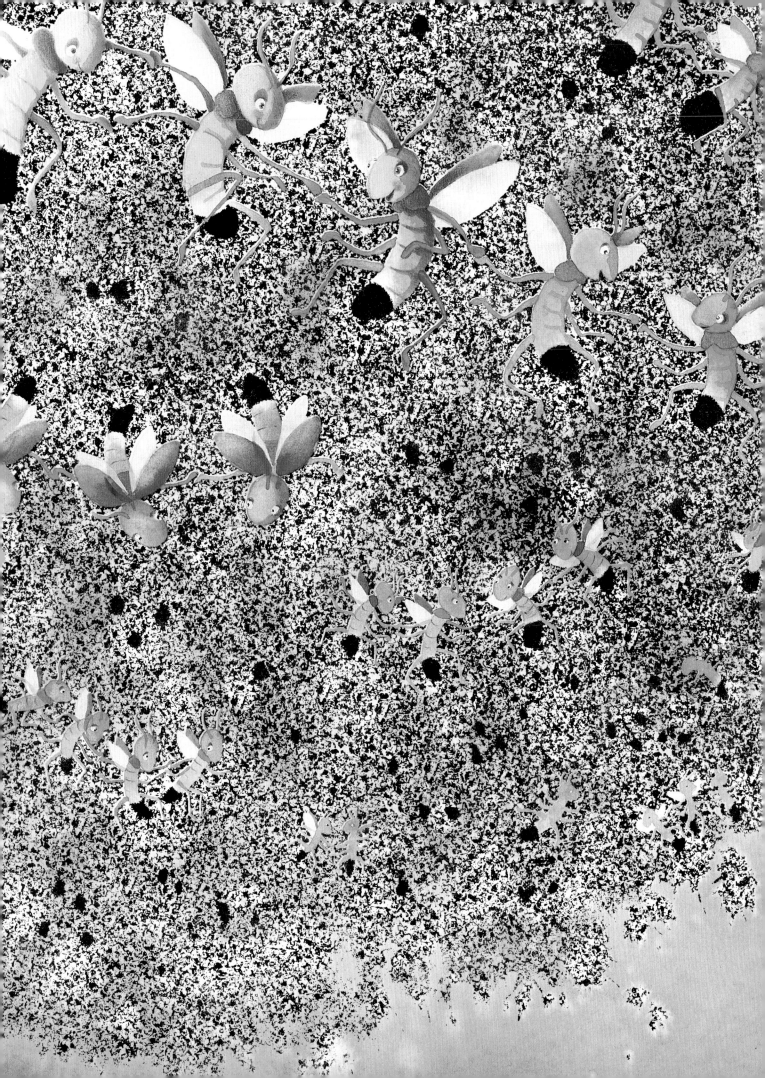

Together their light was so bright,
brighter than the brightest moonlight.
What a wonderful night!
The animals were amazed.
"What a show!" they cried.

Just before morning came, the fireflies broke off in all directions. Now it looked as if there were thousands of dancing, twinkling stars. And with this, the enchanting performance came to an end.

How happy the moon was! Now he knew that when he needed to rest, Nino and the fireflies would take over for him.

Nino thanked the moon, and the moon smiled and said, "Well, Nino, we should always follow our dreams. You see now that if we really want to, we can make the impossible happen. All we must do is work together. Together ANYTHING is possible!"